Salvage

SALVAGE

DAPHNE MARLATT

Red Deer College Press

The Publishers
Red Deer College Press
56 Avenue & 32 Street Box 5005
Red Deer Alberta Canada T4N 5H5

Credits
Design by Peter Bartl/word and image
Typesetting by Boldface Technologies Inc.
Author photo by LaVerne Harrell Clark
Printed and bound in Canada by Gagné Printing Ltée.
for Red Deer College Press

Canadian Cataloguing in Publication Data

Marlatt, Daphne, 1942-
Salvage
Poems.
ISBN 0-88995-074-1
PS8576.A74S2 1991 C811'.54 C91-091245-9
PR9199.3.M37S2 1991

Acknowledgements
The author thanks the editors of the following, in which some of the poems have appeared, sometimes in much earlier versions: *Is, Sound Heritage, Canadian Women's Studies, Poetry Australia, Writers' Quarterly, Credences, line, West Coast Review, The Capilano Review, Diversity,* and *Trois.* "Mauve" and "Character/Jeu de lettres" were first published as two separate chapbooks by NBJ (1985) and Writing (1986) presses, Montreal. They were also included in Nicole Brossard's *A tout regard,* NBJ/BQ, Montreal (1989). "Vacant, lots" and "Seeing your world from the outside" first appeared in *Net Work: Selected Writing,* Vancouver, Talonbooks (1980). "The tri-cornered heart" and "Seeing it go up in smoke" first appeared in *Writing Right: Poetry by Canadian Women,* eds. Douglas Barbour and Marni Stanley, Edmonton: Longspoon (1982). "territory & co." first appeared in *line* 13 (1989).

The author also thanks the Canada Council for a grant in 1986-87, which gave her the time to write and put this book together.

The publishers gratefully acknowledge the financial contribution of the Alberta Foundation for the Arts, Alberta Culture and Multiculturalism, and the Canada Council.

Sources for quotations in:

"River run" from Kim Chernin, "the Hungry Self," an interview published in *East West* XVII, 1, January 1987.
"There is a door" from Sonia Johnson, *Going Out of Our Minds: The Metaphysics of Liberation,* Freedom, CA: The Crossing Press, 1987.
"Reading it" from Susan Squier, "Encountering the Text," *The Women's Review of Books* IV, 2 on David Bleich in *Gender and Reading: Essays on Readers, Texts, and Contexts.* Also from Barbara Walker, *The I Ching of the Goddess,* San Francisco: Harper & Row, 1986.
"Compliments (of the camera" and "Unpaid work" from Marguerite Duras and Xavière Gauthier, *Woman to Woman,* trans. Katharine Jensen, Lincoln: University of Nebraska Press, 1987.
"Park (your) dream" from Lyn Hejinian, "The Supplement," *periodics* 7/8, winter 1981.
"Territory & co." from Dorothy Dinnerstein, *The Mermaid and the Minotaur,* New York: Harper & Row, 1977.
"Booking passage" from *Sappho: A New Translation,* trans. Mary Barnard, Berkeley: University of California Press, 1958.

Contents

Foreword / 9

Salvage / 13
Litter. wreckage. salvage / 15
River run /24
There is a door /26
Reading it /28
Shrimping / 30
Compliments (of the camera / 32
Unpaid work / 34

Passage Ways / 37
An economy of flowers /39
The difference three makes: a narrative /44
Park (your) dream /48
Vacant, lots / 56
Refuse the muse / 58
Seeing your world from the outside / 60
Leaves "the doublet of" / 62
The tri-cornered heart / 63
Seeing it go up in smoke / 67

Territory & co. / 69

Acts of Passage* / 93
Mauve / 95
Character/Jeu de lettres / 103

Booking Passage / 111
To write / 113
(Dis)spelling /114
Booking passage / 115

*Nicole Brossard writes of translation in *A tout regard:*
"La traduction est un acte de passage par lequel une
réalité devient tout à la fois autre et semblable."

Foreword

This book spans two decades, two lifetimes almost, and reaches toward several different communities. The title section, "Salvage," brings the two decades together in a double exposure, with the first "take" consisting of poems from the early seventies when i was writing about Steveston, then a largely Japanese-Canadian fishing community just south of Vancouver on the Fraser River. These poems were subsequently exposed to a second "take" based on my feminist reading and thought of the late eighties and re-read in that light. Most of the poems have changed radically, although, as in a palimpsest, early sentences, even whole stanzagraphs surface intact in these new versions, their "drift" altered in unforeseen directions. Much of "Litter. wreckage. salvage," for instance, stands intact, but interspersed with completely new sections which re-read its subject. Working on these poems felt aquatic: i was working with subliminal currents in the movements of language, whose direction as "direction" only became apparent as i went with the drift, no matter how much flotsam seemed at first to be littering the page.

These are littoral poems, shoreline poems — and by extension the whole book — written on that edge where a feminist consciousness floods the structures of patriarchal thought. They began as a project to salvage what i thought of as "failed" poems. But the entire book attempts to salvage the wreckage of language so freighted with phallocentric values it must be subverted and re-shaped, as Virginia Woolf said of the sentence, for a woman's use.

"Passage ways" moves into the city, the individual poems stemming from particular writing moments uncomplicated by later readings. The first two sequences, meditations on motherhood and how women are situated in a patriarchal sexual economy, were written in the mid and late eighties, with individual women in my life, of differing ages, very much in mind. "Park (your) dream" initiates an earlier series of poems from the late seventies, all written in the heart of Vancouver's downtown on the edge of skid row where i could just afford to rent a writing room for several years. This opens up another economy altogether than the middleclass one, though it's constantly impinged upon by the consumerism of that one.

"Territory & co.," a novella in fragments, represents another layering in time. It began with dream-fragments excised from the first very loose draft of a novel, *Ana Historic* (begun at the same time as the earlier sequence of poems in "Passage Ways") and includes theoretical fragments written more recently, as well as scenes constructed out of diary entries from the late seventies. Like the novel, it turns on an identity play with the name Ana, but unlike the novel, it is situated in residential Chinatown in Vancouver's East End and moves back and forth between the pull of domestic family, on which that community is based, and the alternative pull of a lesbian community of women artists.

The Quebecoise poet and novelist, Nicole Brossard, initiated our exchange of "transformances" with "Mauve" which i translated, adding a coda on the intimacy of the experience of translating. She transformed my play with the letter S in "character" to the letter "L" in her melodic "jeu de lettres." "Mauve," "character/jeu de lettres," and the final section, "Booking passage," were all generated out of a growing sense of community with women writers/readers, drawn by currents of desire in language for contact through time, over space and across cultures.

Daphne Marlatt
March 1991

Salvage

Litter. wreckage. salvage

           below water level, behind — the dyke a road now, back of the wharves, boats, empty sunday / spring,   left with the nets and houses left to dry rot, must, the slow accretion of months as horsetail heads rear out of asexual earth of abandoned gardens brambled

Steveston:

       your women are invisible, your men all gone. Except for a few boats: hey, his spring salmon net's wet. how much you got, Ned? a bucket. thin smile his pride will scarcely allow. WE — got how much you say, Chuck? (pups at the old sea dog.) you stay away with your bucket!

Staying, straying in their individual houses women swim in long slow gleams between blinds, day incessant with its little hooks, its schemes inconsequential finally. They do not look at Star Camp at the company houses broke and broken open — a litter of two by fours, old shingles, bits of plywood forming/   doors torn off their hinges, glass, glass remains of what transparent walls. occasional boot, the wreckage of daffodils someone planted, someone thought to haul in a bucket . . . What matters, mattered once has seeped away. like fluid from a cell, except she keeps her walls intact, her tidal pool the small things of her concern still swim alive alive-oh —

The salmon homing in this season, spring, the sewer out-
falls upstream, oil slick, the deadly freight of acid rain —
she reads the list of casualties in the ongoing war outside
her door.

If *the woman is within,* if that's her place as they have al-
ways said, can she expect her walls not to be broken open
suddenly: Flood, Lightning, Nuclear Light — what attaches
her to the world? dug-up clam, dehoused, who can no
longer bury her head in the sand . . .

ii

fear of the marketplace, of going outdoors. fear of public places, crowds, of leaving home. "the phobia of every day." she trembles like a leaf. has jelly legs. her stomach is a churn, fear stirring her into separate parts: the whip of the superego, the cowering ego, lack of will.

imagine opening your front door and standing on the step. how strong is your fear? relax, take a deep breath. imagine walking down the path to your gate. how strong is your fear now? relax. imagine opening the gate . . .

i want to imagine being in my element, she said.

iii

Fish. paper. (value.) fish. paper. (words, work out to-
wards . . .) an accumulation of desires unbought, nothing
in this world can pay for. I want to walk down the street as
if I had the right to be there, as if it were not their construc-
tion site and stoop, slipping the net of their casting eyes,
slipping the net of their market price. The street belongs
to the men who live *outside,* whose small acts accrete (con-
crete) unspoken claim, a territory that cannot be tres-
passed except you hurry through, for loitering indicates a
desire to be caught,

                    or caught already, prostitute, destitute,
alcoholic, the street is where you swim for smaller fish

                                                        Hey
you! someone fishing for, hey where yah goin? that kick in
the head recognition is, You! something other than fish,
flesh, drowned in the tide line of the unemployable left on
stone planters the city removes

          Whose foot of cement *is* this?

I go fishing too, to bridge that gap i let my line down into
the powerless depths we flounder in where the will (to cap-
italize on things) stands on the opposite side of the street

having made this town, having marked it "No Trespassing"
"No Loitering." No defenses in the smell of beer the private
walls come down, lightfingered, aery as their harmonica,
two young men sprawled in the heat and the young woman
with them, flaunting her being there free, she thinks, for
free —

Fish that escape my line in the swift and surge the street
my feet keep carrying me adrift . . . letting my line fall into
the blank, the mute, defences breached she's letting her
want out there where i am, beached with their receding
ebb.

iv

coping with the world outside. she copes with this and that all day long inside. a successful applicant must be able to cope. she doesn't contend or strive — her struggle is within.

i can't take the bus is the same as i won't take the bus. a failure of will. she says they are staring at her and what will she do without the right change or forgetting to get the transfer when she got on, they stared when he refused, they thought she was dumb. what attaches her to the world? is what repels: the fear of being caught, caught out, caught without —

she doesn't have the words to alter his definition of her.

v

There are no longer any real fish. only a flicker of fish — a movement,

        the baiting you do talking to me in the street, my back against the car and you playing the line, hiding behind the tease i rise to, as to the clover of your smile —

"Fish are there to be caught you know."

Will i rise? school behaviour a herd of fish. just as, back then, swimming through sexual currents looking for eyes, as if they might bridge the gap, flare, romantic semaphore. gone fishing for compliments recognition is, eyes the lure. allure. not looking (out) but looking the look for certain eyes, floating around the places he swam by, i "lost" myself as they say and i did. fall into invisibility, silvered, dead. i floated up and down the school yard with the others, eyes reflecting all they saw, blind to myself, more: hoping to feel that hook when his would connect: "he looked at me!"

All action his, mine merely to be seen. i contend with desire elicited from me, the lure, the bait: i'm worth fishing for.

(How much did he say? the boy, bragging. how much does a fisherman get per pound on spring salmon now?)

The fishy vocabularies we speak our words through. "the fish never says no," you say, the lure speaking. but watch that fish swim right on by. the fish is after something too. something else.

vi

imagine her in her element. not to be taken in its restric-
tive sense as home (is her, closed in).

in her element in other words. blurring the boundary. it's
not that she wants to blur difference, to pretend that out is
in, already past the gate she's past his point of view as cen-
tral (hook/lure) to a real she eludes,

free, she multiplies herself in any woman paces the inside
of her mind her skin half in half out of the common air she
drifts along. casting a thought receives it back this we of
an eye complicit in a smile she gathers fish-quick, taking
the measure of their plural depth she who with every step
and never once (-over).   desires in the infinitive to utter
(outer) her way through: litter.   wreckage.   salvage of
pure intent

River run

　is kept (pent up, hungry) at the edge of boulders rock dam suddenly drops, "letting 'er go," the backedup current streaming river rain and silt from mountains draining . . .

she was not a river nor a man. she stood on the bank, curious, mute, and watched them set out in boats to hunt. she wanted to be among them, not because of the meat they brought in, skilfully secured essentials on the wing, or up, through currents of sea. in the competition between them, in the contest of human skill and animal instinct they were expecting a break, a big one. she thought of women with all that time on their hands as having to bear or care for it, time and its effects on flesh, having to work against it. what was drudgery but the slow expenditure of life? for what? and wasn't she one? *them, their.* she wanted to be on the wing, ride the current, pour with the river's pour out to the mouth . . .

acknowledging this fact that if i'm not this negative female creature . . .

suck and flow, suck and rush, alluvial wash of the river out to meet that which sucks it away from itself . . .

if i'm not this pseudo-man . . .

deft hands, that was what was most noticeable about them, their hands catching up the net with small scissors, knotting, reknotting. their bodies wirey and well used, sure of step, even the older ones who would not easily give up their deck. her they said, and she, speaking of the boats they were married to.

then i'm nothing.

the river they rode. dammed 'er up, he said, to make the channel, two sand flats joined in that alluvial wash swirled back and slowed so well sea brought teredos in with the salt. so they ripped the top of the dam off. at high tide only, high and buoyed by the tide "she" crests on through . . .

she is not a river. she is not a boat.

what's at issue here is whether women can enter the culture AS women.

finding a way to write her in, her and her, write she, write suck and rush, high and daring to be, attaches her body to words where they stick to her licking at old holes, tongue lashings, lashings of rain as at no one. writing their all, splashing around in the muck, allure of the current she rides their rushing out, her and the words all/uvial.

There is a door

There is a door other than that which opens to the known world

drawn in the steamed up windows of the house a house (windows and mouth, lopsided plume) that bares opaque aspects of the soul (no kidding) the way words exit her place of abode, steamed up, where is she anyhow? keeping house as if keeping herself meant hugging a shadowy wall she is playing house without the means with all the right words (keeping it nice) and somehow still feels left outside

he has a full house, three of a kind and a pair no repairing to where she hears he is scaling walls, floodlit

the depression of solitaire: for fear of claws in the legal because (she is tied up inside it all)   believing what they said, that she would die if she went through that door . . .

where women meet where the words face up, are heard — i know what you mean — in these small houses walls are falling

while his back meeting rain on the street slickers into the Buccaneer, relief, the reign of conversation here behind

glass fogged up and closed in it's in-house news exchanged
with change or beer the currency of who makes it here

playing to a small house, house of the ascendant, house of
commons, stars parading through their phrases, stars or
tiny lights —

that there's only so much power, not enough to go round,
to light up windows on the outside of town/the known

the indifferent news —

we are giving up on, moving out of solitaire into a clearer
sense of what relates us, this solar river this windy oikos
simultaneous her sisterfire at the mouth at the mouth
borne inside each of us saying what women see is flooding
out the old inside/outside of our minds

Reading it

so the moon was shining, so what defence was there
against his merriment? "you try so hard," haunting the
wharves at night "to see it"

                              moon a shade off full tonight
past the blackness of this present shed (receding) tide at
ebb's so quiet you hear water drop in water light years
away the two who row into moonglare with their catch or
were they setting a net so far it was hard to see in this
moontrack otherwise black water, lap, a dim outline of is-
land (oars) a little wind the stillness they were drifting in
immense river clearing an immense future (night) ahead of
them, neither behind nor ahead they worked by tide moon
the timing of salmon up against a vague and confused hulk
of boat mast and lights/ hum of some refrigerator plant
from the cannery sheds — "you kill me trying so hard to
see it different — look,"

                              under monoglare off the Esso barge
we stare down on the body of a man sleeping flat out in the
blue of portable tv, "this," he says, "is the real"

so that that is gone, that recessive, that being in among the
home run of salmon, throng on the summit of a dike that
was Water Street violence and competition skimming along
on the prominent

men tend to remain separate from fiction   ·   getting the
catch so as not to get caught (up in) the background only
the setting   for

                    the proposition shifts, a shadowy other-
where leaps at the wharf as the very river's breath hangs
fire — and not impermeable not as if rock doesn't breathe
or water seep into the stock of radioactive waste buried
there in the background dioxin compounds mercury griev-
ing *women   ENTER the world*

                              of the novel jostled sweaty in
the press of so many bodies, men's men's, skirts useless
hampering us in "the feat of passing people without tum-
bling off" the summit of a dike that was water, a hubbub a
thousand names for the no-name *this!* (river) *this!* (light)
this is not what history's after

so the moon was painting in radium real this unreal-ing of
foreground/background where she leans a luminous im-
print paper remembers her, arms brushed with white pear's
awful scent . . . "an old one that, if it could talk would tell
you many things." transplant, she took her stand (*tui*, sea)
in a river of grass flowing over her walk   immersion *as
complete as the pouring of water into water*
                              this is not
background.

Shrimping

stark against the green bushes green water lucent salmon
net, these steamsprayed with tar caught up at the boom
and flowing like a dirge

dirige Domine who hath dominion dominate in techne lord
of the nets

their boats lined up and wearing shrouds of black for the dark
of bottom waters shrimp who do not pray crawl

                                        diminutive
and *shrinking, wrinkled* akin to cabbage with crumpled
leaves acurl where babies, baby shrimp she said look at
them curled in their cans waiting to be picked *crevette,* lit-
tle shrimp, sitting on his fingers stuck up playfully there
and there my sweet looking good enough to eat she was
wearing her short dress with frilly underwear, so pink this
little crack crevasse (la la) we have taken over this fissure
in the gender of it all

                        this fiction pink for little girls that we
were the ones plying the net, fore-ply alive in the redden-
ing of desire from the raw to the cooked dressing her femi-
nine with just a bit of sauce, you don't want to look like a
boy do you? widening the gap (crevasse) a finger's width

just letting her know what's him (fishing) for her below

and the net goes roaring with the lead weight of it dead
weight down to unseen dark her body crawls feathery legs
(undrowned) feathery head light barely makes out the
splurr and creep of net in the tone of his words my little
shrimp

the name of the net   the name of the net   the name of
the net   later she cannot dredge it up at all.

Compliments (of the camera

what she's fishing for, wishing there outside the hair-
dresser's on an ordinary street, hair erased by her chiffon
scarf old ski jacket flattened now or faded she faces the
camera faces up to being there and not about to go in or
out with this evasive tilt to her head she's standing not
quite square smile reined in at the corners her eyebrows
hope —

trailing a baited line o let me like my look like this is what
you get, the small fish of an idea slipping the hand

this blank where fear settles in she is not quite sure she is
not ordinarily traversed by, the street its emblems of de-
sire this man in the form of a camera does not take the hole
where eyes were

      (hers, fishquick

hooked and dressed secure there in the ordinary

years of it, what comes down: the side of his hand slapping
her into a shape she resists — stilled fish. yet the eyes

                                            blink
getting used to the taste of fear as that which squirms alive

on the hook o she is sure she exists in the downward slice
of his hand unshutt(er)able up — no, not up, it's a lateral
movement fish make, *nothing goes anywhere, but things
move . . . that's not where it's dangerous; it's when you're
trying to get out you see*

a lot on your plate lifted out of the socalled order of things
face to face with the hole you've been fishing for

Unpaid work

cloud so low a sort of pearlgrey nothing houses across the
road silhouette against this no-seam settling everywhere
darker imperceptibly late the rain osmotic world a sort of
sponge taking it in seeping out they sit two women in a
darkening room

won't let it stop her you know   doesn't trust doctors
she'll go on dancing despite them

a surf breaking mitral up through the heart the same old
ebb and flow   thuds back down

and her baby, what of him? to sort it out, dancing her life
through the fog on the edge of its lifting abandon aban-
donment o the complex heart with its too much blood
forced up this hole in the afternoon after the chores after
the afterwords and facing emptiness this lack of meaning
she is dancing through their hearts a small banner waving
ban to speak publicly of this   ·

    *. . . how to keep a woman from feeding a child when he's
hungry.* (and could you?)

it would be an incredible crime not to do it.

and do you think we'd have to get to the point where we wouldn't do it?

the mother, the mothers beginning to speak of the daughter abandoned already, a sorter of small seeds houseworker head bound out of sorts (destiny) dancing her way beyond anatomy

in a sort of pearlgrey nothing houses across the road silhouette against this no-seam settling everywhere they sit two women in a darkened room striking words and lighting them

she refuses to listen . . . *do we have to refuse everything? . . . I don't know, it's a thing we've never tried.*

Passage Ways

An economy of flowers

in full bloom they said seeing me large as a pod, a fruit,
ripe and already taken. the mother flowers in me. hy-
drangea. blue as a virgin gone to seed.

*it was a sort of grace, she felt, that had brought her life to
such fruition. despite the nausea, the weeks in bed mysteri-
ously and anxiously bleeding. memories of being hit by a
truck, an earlier tearing loss that felt like giving death. this
one was delivered by loving hands, blue flower squalling
with feet still rooted in her mother's body. she felt like a
child herself she said, emotion washed clean of doubt. cry-
ing with child, with her child: with her was the miracle. she
was going to bury the placenta that had seen them through,
plant a hydrangea in it.*

40

the mother spoils: blue as the Virgin's cloak(ed) in memo-
riam habit yes, as if she didn't wear the same dowd day in,
out (it doesn't matter or who's to see?) or it's earth colour
and we are back to who takes us all in eventually.

*beige slippers with tatty fur trim she slops around in the
colour of last year's blooms turned tan now in the wind or
fragile-eaten by all manner of days she keeps talking about
the Isle of Man she keeps saying someplace they bloom the
size of a man's head, or is it dinner plates? she carries the
memory around a round the overblown one her body is.
the plates have chips, are losing their flowers under over-
use. she says the kids are at her all the time, the tiny fillet
of gold leaf gone.*

she. sheets and the nice entice. like spring she said i always thought it happened in orchards of apple blossom. boudoirs of blue sheets. (or that was the other story getting pregnant if he kissed you.) red blossomed on my slip on the floor of the ferry's much travelled carpet under my back, feet of oblivion walking by on deck. that was the fruit of beer drinking she'd have said.

sitting in the shopping mall amid her spoils. blue shirt. green eye shadow. sitting in the smell of Tabu. Fidgi fidgetting. green eye smiling over tan-skinned muscle-fitness tone. ready it sings to meet him, any him she is in the market for.

hydrangea. water vessel. from the cuplike shape of its pod. mother flowers. the ones they put razor blades under to turn them blue.

that one wears tiny zippers in her ear. words a warning, labels to be taken, outrageously. Mad ma(i)d mad(e) her cultural collaboration in a real that violence co-opts she's at the ready. lean as a whip, quick as plastic, incendiary.

mother is not desire but the registered mark of ownership.
initiated in a system of exchange, she is the visible mark,
the easy drupe. dowd, *doude* (slut). "slit." once picked. in
the monoculture.

The difference three makes: a narrative

for Mary S.

in the dream we argued about a preposition as if in French
Emily held the key to the whole story.

you wanted it to read: The Family of Emily Courte is Tired
from *The Family of Emily Courte is Tired* — how do we
translate?

not that i remember translating so much as turning the
page in a kind of hungry absorption and then backing up
to reflect, as one does, about the message of the title, i
thought — (this was all about framing, for instance the
kind of framing a table of contents does) — what's the
point of repeating, je me tue à vous le répeter (how many
times?) unless it's of . . . tired of . . .

"the family romance."

because the bed had framed you/us watching her slide out
into this room so full of women and her father too. three
midwives three wise women around your Mary. three the
beginning of family, Emily at the end . . .

there's a chapter within the book from which it takes its

name you explained, as the child does the family. or the family does the child i thought. it wasn't Emily that stopped short.

an alley walled by buildings on three sides. this was not in the table of contents.

the house on the hill will be sold, the house you brought her through snow to. lying in sun on the carpet to cure her yellow, sucking white, and the deep content of night out in the country she was not to be brought up in. so there is the letting go of leaves of strawberry begonias, spider plant, the deck, the dogs . . . he wanted out so you moved.

this book, turning the pages tabled there, coupé Court(e). the book that Emily cannot read she is the title page for.

alone no solace, alone the symbiosis of two — pre-mirror, pre-frame. don't drop it: there is that fear you have, of not being able to carry her all alone.

the family is Emily but Emily is more.
Emily short with the short-sightedness of the small sleeps in her crib, blonde hair splayed in her court of little pigs (3) bears (3) the little train that could, dream the family dream of inheritance in her, in her irritants not the dream that could soothe her at all.

this was all about framing as a border frames the contents of the title page where rights are displayed. beyond design designation under the sign of famililacae: nothing so pure as a lily . . .

denying her her father he charged when you moved to the city where the difference three makes became apparent in the helping of friends. at the end of the alley sometimes you turn around.

(f.) Emily out of family. tabled.
in a trice (this is not nice Emilology) en trois coups de cuiller à pot stirred up in the social she comes out little dresses little rag doll tout Court(e) hands full of the train of them repeating tired so tired of the long sanctification in which she appears daddy's angel girl.

the difference three makes always this cry in the night as you return from your fear to find her calling daddy, name for the third person standing by who can pry her loose from the overwhelming two, tu. you teach her big girls don't nurse. let me hold it mama. the languaged mouth as one little pig went to market, one little first person one.

third person could be anyone when it comes to that.

the story says paternal–I, don't rock the stable.

for the Word is His she will write as I distinct from mother-mine-o-lode, turning away in the script that writes her out of the reciprocal and into what she will become when narrative begins its triple beat about, about her/accusative.

this is all about framing.

Park (your) dream

never stationary, was
from the first rolling down
hill
      even in white
      despite
      words
         call you

         back intact un
         toucht ad
         mirable small
         giraffe
            perambulating
         always affable
         your mother's eye

no, it was wild
monkey cries midair
whole troupes leaping trees leaping
      destiny

         to fly like that

         despite intent, to
         roll unceasingly

dizzy and free to the
ends of the
earth

~

park (enclosed
domestic

safely
tranquillized

white jacket
boos the moment
she wants to be happy

"bougain/
villea, you will
smell it, girl," it
doesn't smell

trans
posing relics into dis
ordered sense or

paradise between firs
glistening (furs in a
black-suit setup

    (and over the wall?

dummy trunk between
two crushed petals

    was her body ever
    present?

        DANGER SIGN

park your dream, she said
in the mind

(they wave a bottle

where it belongs

~

park for love
flowers

fir
      /st
            carnation
            (stolen off a song
            didn't know it
            was the streets'

                  vine, cypress, yew
                  houses you knew

                  a white
                  sports coat, hardly

                  tradein denim, leather-
                  jackets dying
                  all over our house this
                  time of year we

                  share the moon, briefly
                  walking powell street
                  grounds

~

parked

      out in the sun
      part dream
      stranded by happenstance
      or will
          (to let
                any habitant
                    inhabit

wilful traffic strands
them in pigeon park without
whatever it takes
          (belief, say

      hi speedy
      where ya goin?
          (so fast

              suspect

    holes in the eye in
    the   their   my
    intent

hours, and ours
inhabiting
the common day

~

paradise

the movement is backward
back to hyde park
and pan (peter even

    enclosed
    eden, experience
    there in the form of a
    drunk

        (what does he bring?
        what other
        ways to seem

free, and so close in to hell
she said, a wraith, a wrath to us

he can only be
perfectly trusting

curled on the ground
in the open, fast
asleep

"you ever seen a woman
do that? she'd never be left
alone"

(only
sifting the
streets for her
imaginary
soul

(watchful
what lies
there

to make it, take it, break it
anger in the form of iron
filings rose

whatever's left

we are likely to find ourselves
pondering suchness as the
essence of bourgeois
memorabilia –L.H.

                    clarity and a
magnetic tongue, the lyric
transpose

syntax of old alleys, old
passageways of *pairi-daēza*

climbing the walls even
to get over it

Vacant, lots

of vacant lots vegetation fills: dandelion, tansy in tall spokes, small clover only those close to the ground will see in seedy grasses waving off sandhill lots they weave, waving a bottle,   *hey!   come on over.* sun-struck, drowsy and raucous, sun fuming the wine in their heads. vacant over sidewalk, weaving up against telephone poles . . . *can't do it, man. i'm a good man,*   or. *my name is mud . . .*

no wires over vacant lots. no connection calling them back. home this moment, these small flowers, this much satupon mud worn into backsides of hills they view the city from, its increment of meaning every hoarding, every passing bus leaks, non-sense, a verbal inflation that standardizes the value of words

shut up, shut UP, he yells, into the open air signs fill, everywhere. they want to fill up the vacant lot he is, a hole in the system words won't fill.   fill in the grass. full with friends camped in a ring around a bottle — on vacation we say (see vacant, see empty of work).   empty (pay, pay). and a fight erupts.   someone stoned is left alone.   vacant, we say of eyes deprived of sense (our sense), except for nightmare: always someone climbing on somebody

else's neck   for a bit more air. always these holes in our-
selves or where we are

                              battered and bleeding.   so few
words, worry beads in the mouth, accrue value   being
tongued over and over   *go fuck yourself,* or,   *THERE's a
friend*   (in need)

"hey," he sez, with the broken arm by the liquor store. i
think what for? small change? "you vote NDP or," lifting
his cast, "i'll club you over the head." and the grin runs
somewhere between me and his buddies who rock back on
their heels and applaud.

                              votes get cast. silently in vacant lots
the terms run free. dying into the grass, these men kill the
system in themselves/themselves ghosts of the open air.

Refuse the muse

baby's breath? bridal wreath? it's not spirea blowing intent
away the minute skins're sucked   *just trash — I lOve it*   by
day's breath passing   eyes   take in these petals   white,
drift off cementblock wall   off topless legs in chino,
denim   YOU WILL BUY ME   nothing short of

                                             aim / intent,
the almost fragrant stink of pollen   "junk was here" it sez
in the telephone booth   in the shirt off her back   *if not
for you*   intent on the rest of her drift . . . "you filthy
hounds!"

             Ripley's male hips wellhung   limbs to a traffic
lingerers   hangers-on all windows eyes

                                        it's not meadow-
sweet   (how hack it?) sticks   TRY ME ON FOR SIZE

street's a mouth (forget) anyone enters, anyone walks a
story down to the nearest pub and enters, leaving rain
outside, small sounds, the hour (white, a shedding of
words inaudible)   all of the hour attends   how
money gets spent, on whom, or where it comes from   his-
tory the man said, "someone's particular story"   (and *I
wasn't)* "what's your line?"

. . . *born with much,* just the street some words
and such   all of what's ours he might have scoffed, claim-
ing her   the, a   poem (looking good) turn up

to keep her coming (eyes), keep talking   til she walks
right in, tries him on for size

                              this drift flourishing round his I's

Seeing your world from the outside

                                        outside night, light,
absence is whirling down   down the order of night, not
upside, out — alleyways, all ways the walls say no.

standing inside your world is full of holes   floating doors:
"a scream is an appraisal."   you   apprised of what we
see are messages off walls

                        and let me read the black tint un-
der your eyes from banging your head all night against the
wall of your own want   "salud! ladies of the night"   who do
not win *(Express yourself)*

                    Do Not phone.

                            Do Not move on to Go.

this game is rigged   because somebody has to be at the
bottom,   lottery system,   lots have to be at the bottom so
somebody else comes out on top.   everybody wants.   and
chance is the midnight bus with the winning number: will
it stop where you stop? is this the right spot? is this a stop
at all?   STOP.

the night is full of losers and empty buses, palisades of

light adrift, nosed in to the curb, some slight collision, lights still on, sits under neon, nothing left to lose. black are the scrawls of want on the walls that do not see us ("annie was here") to be lost ("take me home") in want, o baby, *will you still feed me? will you still need me?*

black and white.   and you.   standing inside your world photographing doors or holes in the wall night pours through.   "a scream is an appraisal."   you.   a scream is a refusal.   we.   refuse to keep in all that silence pressing through the walls, o women, women who write

"because the night belongs to us"

Leaves "the doublet of"

"attached,"   trees rain beats down   rainbeats down the
street, dark   would beat them off   leaves, attached and
free, whirl   attacked   tacked, not nailed to the tree
they're dancing from, as on, in   leaf up through the stem,
slender petiole a stalk or little foot

                              and when the blood ebbs
back, and when the sap falls back into the bole of the tree,
so cold i struggle to remember   how the leaf cleaves, that
attachment through the slender   stalk, stalked in dark-ness
you hide, mute, i catch at   you, stand next to, quiver

and you sway still listening to it   street news in the dark
rush by   and gone, we whirl so slow, so slow on the one
stalk   attacked and doubting and attached

The tri-cornered heart

at-tract: asparagus fern in my eye its one wood cherry
clinging, will, long after the fragrant flowers are gone, be
drawn, am drawn. and not by clinging.

it's not a "frailty of will," yours and the drunks on Powell —
hapless you said, helpless you meant, vagrant. it's when
the rains come not to water flowers (they do) but drizzle in
your eye the misery of self gone vacant.

to you and you, two you's. from "the used heart."

bring me in, out of the rain this perfect yellow tulip open-
ing in the warmth of kitchen (irresistible) to full, spread,
glory of lemon (ha, quick intake of breath, hh, in the heart
of, lemon) smudges at the base of what you call this tri-
cornered heart, green, this stark geometry.

hearth: with the missing h of heart, sound shifter. earth
and a breath beginning.

two-way streets transform overnight traffic flows one way
in the attempt to unblock the heart. congestion. volley-
ing. cars desires ride, images in our eyes. will make you.
want — what? want.

to want the moon: that abstract rock.

a note said your studio had been broken into and when i
phoned i was told a drunk had fallen through. shards of
glass and blood. fallen into the empty hole of your lens
where no photograph exists. he wasn't notified of risks.
he went his way in a city ambulance and now there is a
hole where he was.

the hole in your heart where love sounds a breath out into
what is.

lost in the taking of it. *in the love stirred by photography is
pity.* for what has been.

the eye and the heart. slightly crazy in their synapse. crazy
walking downtown last night. down the welfare street of
disembodied strangers reeling under a moon demateriali-
ized, violent and pissing in desperate reassurance of the
familiar. sirens go all night. the sirens in your head all
right. fences and windows blowing with the cold, gone
open, gone naked, stepping slowly through the hole in the
plate glass window, snatching the biggest fish to cradle
(blue lips again). gone empty, gone mirror, gone looking
thanks.

want hurts. want implies a lack in what has been. the avocado wants water. and light. and earth. each day all over again.

we want it simple, all the ways we lean on each other, love/ to be counted on. as home, that place you belong. turn off the light and lock the door. while the world grows wild outside, the other face of desire (turn, turn to the moon), a complex paranoia breeds radioactive flowers, the poverty line, accretion of numbers that bleed us white.

inconsolable. uncontainable, in the spread of our being here. in the flesh. flayed.

overnight petal skins went silvery lost and fallen into the sink, at sixes and three. at the lip/ what is left,   a three-lip womb. larger now and nude, exuding one clear drop, one tiny bleeding sound.

heart, *eart.* 2nd person singular between the sound of heart, the sound of hearth. me in you. and you.

people are not flowers, last longer, die longing. for what's wanted leans visibly like a flower or a lemon tree on the other side of the fence.

origin obscure. *límún,* not something eggshaped and yel- low, thing to hold. no thing but a ringing sound we move

in, gleam or glowing drawn in wild flows, wild (yellow)
flowers outward (in that moment

juice:

let me take you apart, you said. and the room dark, piano
silent under the return beat of rock.

Seeing it go up in smoke

"as if"
what happens is only the flare of a cigarette. he is smok-
ing. she is watching *summer and smoke*. they have driven
through the valley in a haze of summer sharing the silence
of twilight. the silence is sharing or. silence is a screen be-
tween, silence reflects what does not get said. the appar-
ent silence of two heads looking out of each its own space

"as if nothing"
were happening he might have thought, toward the light
his camera shares, a going intent, having brought the
mask that makes his face an inner room. they had rented
the room, had viewed it, viewed the bed and tv screen she
had already imagined, taking his mask which is an image
of himself as the outer face of a movie she is trying to si-
lence in her head. the way words keep moving it is sup-
posing. what might he make of it, what he has seen, and
has she seen behind (a screen) his image of it?

"nothing untoward"
he means toward her he does not reveal intent but lets it,
whatever that is, happen. as it happens her listening to,
but she is also watching, the talkies he once said she is
given to, given over completely he means taken over by,
this incessant ripple of motive: will she? does he? have

something else in mind? stretched out on the bed she is
intent on following the reach of their desire. does he think
she wants to fill up the silence between? or does she think
smokescreen, seeing him compose in silent frames that
other movie he is making, the tv screen a part of what he
composes, his nudity opposes (it, her, them). speaking
thus to her, or speaking to his camera? like summer's go-
ing up

"were"
he says toward their watching where they are going, don't
mind me, meaning (a)side or (un)toward meaning nothing
is happening but him (nude) and her (fully clothed) watch-
ing him masked, or the mask and him, take place else-
where she has fallen between. she was not there where he
was watching himself watch her watching summer smoke
in some imagined south they have not entered where, be-
hind the mask and silently, desire is to be viewed

"happening"
between and out of it she feels is it but it is, the camera
making it happen. pull the plunger will you, he says, in the
blink of an eye that takes her where he has posed himself
at the edge of her attention. is he the movie then? he is
the making, and making it opposes her viewing what is
made, though in seeing it she is remaking a movie that
goes on viewing itself in the smoke of being unseen "as if
nothing untoward were happening"

Territory & co.

Territory & co.

it was the way they kept taking his joke and playing with it, making it a familiar part of their exchange, knock knock. who's there? and then a word, some ordinary obvious word like banana or tank capitalized, her son would capitalize on the exchange and back again, T'ank you. it was the unacknowledged door all of it got said through that intrigued her. why can't he or she just open it? for the joke, he said, and dummy rhymed with mummy — you have to talk to each other, right? i mean you can't just *see* it's not, it's not who? Van. Van? couver the eggs will you. that's not one. why not? you made it up, he chimed in on her son's behalf.

no i didn't, it's what he does when she's giving birth you know, couvade, they do that in some societies. and they were off on their own, their grownup game now. well you can't blame him for wanting to keep all his eggs covered. *his* eggs? oh you mean he has to know they're his? of course. what if there's some stranger knocking? isn't that the point? there's always some stranger knocking at the family door.

and anyway, she thought, it always feels stranger when it comes to claiming territory. after all they were only playing . . . clearly it's all about naming, he said.

naming and framing. this is beginning to sound like an old story. you mean familiar — well, they weren't a family until they left. got thrown out, after she did what she did to cause it, all that loss, all the animals and plants he'd named except the two that had already been named, with capital letters. and just 'cause she got curious, right? and then they left and she kept giving him new ones to name. and he kept track, he told the story, he passed it all on, father to son, desert camp to town.

who was Hastings anyway? i don't know, he sounds very British. that was another capital letter. he got a mill named after him and then this street and if it hadn't been for Vancouver himself . . .

it's the name of the game, he said, butting his cigarette like a form of punctuation. terri-stories.

it's what she loved about where they went in conversation. at night they slept not far from that street and she dreamed it before it was even named. she feels it hold her body present in the whisper the wispy arms of cedar and other coniferous beings hold the clearing. she is one small part of. not even conscious she is dreaming. brush. soft. stroke. fir. by a hair. here. "let all these present show their naming . . ." she tosses undecided, not knowing whether to stay where the small lamps are or cross the border into unnameable dark.

~

in her reading certain phrases have the habit of sticking
and she carries them around with her like magic stones. to
toss into the blank of the page and watch what they leave
widen:

> . . . *pre-verbal euphoria,* . . . *effortless bodily bliss* . . .

but though she carries them with her they are someone
else's, not hers, they stick out like tiny pebbles in the wash
of her daily words.

~

she tries on secret names as if she might be someone other
than her — when she sits at Eleni's table, for instance, not
in place or unsure of her place or not sure she isn't out of it
when they discuss words — Ana Choristic. Eleni can flash
them and bend them and sometimes it is charm, now in-
cantation she is drawn by, Eleni's black hair that hides the
inadmissible in her eye, the fury of her voice, melodic as if
she were singing. Eleni has thrown out pictures, plants,
has stripped her walls to orient herself in space, bare of

the accumulation, the acculturation of what denies her in
her habitat. it depends what counts for you, she says, and
whether you do.

~

she has named it and tried to tame it but that doesn't
change anything. Ana Choristic not Ana Chronistic — the
moveable "are" they are moving her out of place.

~

and the dream isn't telling she thinks. i'd driven off with-
out him as i've pretended to do when he's dawdled, but
this time i let myself forget — how could i?

it was all the other things in my head which run on like the
news, like tickertape, like a road leading to a foreign land-
scape. like the road he and his pal ambled oh so slowly
down, munching their chips, one long ketchup-covered
straw after another, and where would it end? i walked fast
ahead, got in the car, veered out and drove towards them,
in part to save time, in part resenting their refusal to be-

lieve in it. it was me that ran out on time and left, pretending not to see them and feeling what it would be like to just drive straight ahead, leave it all behind. they waved, hey! hi! big joke. i stopped of course.

but that night i drove on driving on erased him from my mind, a new landscape, very hilly, on top of one of those hills a park and the animistic scent of flower beds where strange blooms lie hidden, trees insisting their presence in the dark, frisson for me in the car taking a turn down a steep hill i'm suddenly on inner city streets, rundown houses and down-at-the-heel corner store, newspaper blowing, beer sign in the window neon wink, tv light in rooms receding shadowy enough to have been mansions in their once uptightness falling softly apart and kids running free on bikes playing sidewalk games in the dusk that light he loves when anything seems possible when you're out in it after hours and what you might see you were not meant to —

these subliminal stories. what is narrative but the burden of an emotion the writing labours under, trying to recover, uncover, this thing about to be hatched?

why does she choose Ana Mystic in this verbal sparring match while he, he wants to name the game, lay alternate bets in the heart of the city.

she asked him what he thought it meant, Territory. what
you think you own, he said, from the land around a town to
what the town uses up. no, she said, i mean the heart of
the city. and lighting up another he tossed his match into
the ashtray she was toying with. what's anyone's word?
what's anyone worth?

~

tomatoes, she writes. ripe tomatoes. sound vaguely like the
fifties. in this block she thinks anything sounds like the
fifties. hot tamata. whereas hers at the end of the lot will
soften, go slowly red late afternoon Indian summer haze.
the length of the alley houses opening, doors, windows
dazed in that anachronistic heat. even so, there's a chill as
the light goes, around five, furtive as a cat slipping between
the sheds.

and even so, red, they are not, my tomatoes as red as the
weathered garage opposite. whose? it only says in great
black letters TOM DELVECCHIO faded now NO DUMPING,
and there is no Italian left on that side of the block to claim
his word. mostly huddled, brightpainted, rotting softly in
the light these walls hold up the eaves of Chinatown. and
to my neighbour with black umbrella on a sunlit day, mak-
ing her way to the vegetable market, i am the odd one out.

~

Ana, Ana Mnesis. a complete case history, as in she was a
case. who? 'case you don't believe me. going on making
them up, day in day out. is this in the developmental books
age nine, as predictable a phase as crawls, stands without
support, takes first steps. part of the plotted territory we
stumble through? as for age thirty-six — ?

~

at loose ends, he says, when the work doesn't come, as if
the story had unravelled, loosefitting and ragged about
the edges. at loose ends we never sit on the stoop, like we
used to, looking at what we inhabit.

i'm twisting odd strands together, finding likely ends to
knot, not for my own, which seem unknown to me as my
other he standing there, legs sturdy and longer every day,
hoisting the knapsack over his shoulder, announces i'm
running away.

but why? because you're always telling me what to do.
(treading on someone else's territory, sonny?) so let him

go, he says, let him find out what it's all about, the world so full of knocks and he so full of himself.

(knock, knock. who's there? putsch. putsch who? putsch yer money where yer mouth is.)

talking tough, enough to take on the wide world. it takes money they said, *get a job,* for you to be taken seriously. someone of substance means someone of independent means not a self unravelling in the wind of their direction and expectation.

~

i said when she asked, i feel at home here, but that was pre-sumptious as she who is also white and has likewise moved around a lot could tell. i meant i seem to recognize the generosity of this light, the long peopled evenings, children racing their shadow selves in the dusk — from where? i meant it's familiar yes, but not mine, though we are allowed to be here in it.

having tucked him up with the cat and watched him stretch out light in that weightless place just under the roof, i walked out into the killdeer's cry, i walked out in my slippers down the alley to the park and wept at the drinking fountain, worn benches, worn branches of the much-climbed pine in its bed. kids, rubbies, dogs — traces only. all night long water slides from distant mountains into the throat of the pipe, all night long it rises gurgling its elemental sound in the dark . . .

~

it doesn't matter, he said, as if the terms of their argument were nothing at all (and if that were so, how talk? how even know where each stood?). look, he said, holding up his hand, see those gaps? holding it up so she could see light shine in the spaces between his fingers. that's who i am, i can't even hold a handful of sand without it trickling through, and money means even less to me. these words were meant to answer her tilting at the discrepancy between what each could make, would make — in the argument between them.

those were his final terms then? — the terminal move of a fridge, which she'd never questioned, faced only with the difficulty of helping him move something that big. and he, not taller than she, dressed like a mover in carpenter's overalls, did move, fast, sliding their fridge with the lightfoot energy his sentences took, shifting them onto new territory.

no, they were in some lobby of a Grand Hotel, abandon meant Grand, where the fridge had to go against the far wall. hang onto it, he said, because he wanted to pull the rug out from under, his favourite rug with a border of sardines woven in blue. she was holding up the fridge so how could she see when he showed her what she was taking her stand on?

~

transport, Eleni said, is one of the nouns i like that move across borders, it's subversive, a mini-truck of pure delight. she was watching Eleni's mouth move its freight of words. green light? she laughed. they both drove, though in the city Eleni, with very little money, took buses, read library books. transport was easy, it was when Eleni said that being with a woman was mythological she balked.

that's so literary, it's a stereotype i wouldn't think you'd use. Eleni, whose imagination was fueled by a metaphysic of words, using *mythological* and gazing out the window, face not *veiled* — refusing, refusing to be read. mouth, she said, it goes back to mouth, look it up. and then getting up, making tea with familiar gravity. pause. what do you mean? as if that were all she could say. and anyway she knew that etymology. Eleni was talking about Luce and Judith, the currents that crossed the borders of their individual lives. how she knew when to or when not to phone, how Luce knew when she was being dishonest, how her words appeared in Judith's dream and Luce's images in hers — and it's not just them, other women friends who are with women artists too. it's as if we are tapping something old and communal, as if the limits between selves are only fiction and we actually live inside each other's thought.

she was watching Eleni's mouth which was different from hers, the way those lips met at the end of a phrase, their fullness touching and slowing each other, parting as the words came in little spurts — this notion of my work or yours . . . we don't need to own . . . and were all her other friends her lovers too?

~

soft tomatoes. seeding and nodding into place. low moon. slow feet, soft, soft. walking out in it to be part of it. post-partal and yet. not the dearly departed, she is looking at

gardens and rot, the slow process of weather incremental
to sunny situation, whether or not hers is any different, is
not so much the point, walking horizontal here as long slow
beams of moonlight walk her by the rooms of other lives.

~

but there are those mythical beasts again. bêtes noires.
she was in the midst of a conversation, an ordinary con-
versation about cooking something or other for the people
they were having over, all the usual alternatives of this or
that depending on time and everyone's taste. and there
they were when she turned and glanced out the window
onto what looked life Africa, a dry stretch of skin, a few
wispy trees (mimosa maybe) rubbed bare by their looming
hides the colour of mud. she was afraid of their size, the
mammoth size of their heads which leered and grinned.
were they destructive? could someone lead them away
without being killed?

and there was Judith in the dust, back turned to her, black
scarf held at arm's length. elegant in jeans, she was danc-
ing alone in the dust of mammoth beasts who on their
pointed hooves were dancing with her.

one exposure of the mind's eye. overexposed the way that dust filled the background, up in heaven too, sky. but the blackness of her scarf an extension of the slim darkness her body made, so dark even the animals receded, leering and grinning heads, shaggy manes, man in his cave. peering out of the smoke at an idea.

i leave my hand on all this, Judith said, to show it is a true story, painted at night in the sleeping quarters for all those little heads who wondered where the others went.

~

she was puzzling over *the earliest . . . , the unqualified animal-poetic mode . . . .* more stones.

~

she had painted home as a picture. coming up the path under the maple tree and up the steps she had painted, she opened the door on something incomplete.

nobody home? it was silent — no movie music, no gun battle raging. well, it's not nobody, he yelled from another room.

so *somebody's* here?

i mean it's not just *anybody,* he pursued.

he was with himself then, not lost at all. good, i wouldn't want to think that nobody was off somewhere and somebody was nowhere.

sauntering into the room he explained with pre-pubescent clarity: nobody's nowhere and anybody's anywhere so somebody's got to be somewhere, right?

that was him. talking his way right out of her skin.

~

i was sitting with someone i liked. i was sitting with someone i'd known so long and we liked each other so well we were almost married and yet, there were still things to declare. more borders, more border crossings. the state, he said, co-opts our desire into hard currency, the standard of exchange that will maintain it. he was owing not owning but owning up to it when he said, and we all subscribe to this shit.

~

perhaps she is not so much unhappy as confused. by the words and what they do and don't mean (when to, or when not to phone). she wants to call them up, her magic stones with the words cut in, inscribed, but even as she shifts them in the light to read one way, the way she thinks she understands, they shift into another.

~

she was with Luce who was saying, but the dark is where we live. sitting opposite her at the table, Eleni and Judith on the long side opposite them. sitting in the particular smell of Luce's kitchen, homey and comfortable in the musty building that was always up for sale. the table stood against the wall where Luce's photos hung, clipped to a string by odd corners.

no, the dark is what we refuse to name. with that remark she felt closer to Eleni who was not so much opposite as beside her, placing her mug of tea on the much marked table. a table with a history she thought, tracing old scars, old burn marks there.

Judith had said about one of the faces on the line, indistinct in the shadow of blinds like bars disappearing at its outer edge, your dark side shows. just as she'd been wondering whose face it was, Luce's imaging of herself imprisoned there, or Judith's gaze taken through the strictures of taboo. there wasn't much left except the unknowable gaze. a face in the dark. as she was.

that's one way, Luce was saying, of seeing its power. around them the white walls with their shards of mirror caught pieces of them sitting there — from where she sat, pieces of Luce. we refuse to recognize our power and so we go on cutting each other down to size.

power? Judith laughed sardonically, is too simple. either you have power or you're in someone else's.

Luce's return was swift, and flat. you don't have anything, she said staring down at her tea. or anybody, if you want to really look at it.

in the silence that followed she glanced at Eleni who avoided her gaze. Judith was tipping her chair back and staring at the wall with an amused expression.

she had to go, she really had to be getting home, and she should offer Eleni a ride back to their side of town, but wasn't that presuming? assuming Eleni would be leaving soon? and who was she to know? the silence still hummed between them when she said, i've got to go . . .

Luce gave her a cold stare. why are you so unfree?

she stopped. what do you mean?

you always say you have to do this or that as if you're not responsible for wanting to. you want to go.

no i don't, she said, it's just that i have to, it's getting late and i have to get home. under the image of him coming back from school to find her gone, she was evading something she knew Luce would name, could, in an instant —

they were watching her begin to recognize the words Luce hat not uttered. you've come too far.

~

i dreamt about you finding an egg, she said. isn't that funny when you were once an egg in me?

no, he said, i wasn't an egg. i was a sperm.

knock knock, she said, that was your dad. and you were once an egg too. anyway you found this egg, all grey and wrapped in bandages. i guess it was a mummy of an egg. you showed me where you'd made a nest for it in the driveway behind a parked truck. i said that's not a good place, it'll get run over there. but you weren't worrying, you just left it, so then i had to scoop it up out of the sand.

what do you mean i just left it? i didn't care about it?

i guess you didn't think the truck was worth worrying about. anyway i realize you must have left it there because the sand was warm and good for hatching. so i bury it further up on the side of the road in the same sand, and then i see that the pointed end which had been sticking out is moving. i dig it up again and out comes this tiny cartoon figure of a white rooster like the rooster in the chicken hawk comic, but this one's so tiny the grains of sand are knocking him over. i pick him up and he's connected to my fingers by invisible threads. i know i have to feed him, make him grow, so i take him to the forest ranger's tower which is a sort of doctor's office. the doctor asks me, does he know who he is? and i say, well look at the way his toes curl under, anyone can tell who he is. and i point to him in the doorway where he's standing, a huge gawky teenager. i call him Goofy.

oh mum, you've got the comics all mixed up.

sardines and eggs.

~

it's not just anybody she will open to. Ana Leptic. restora-
tive. Ana Thema, this double she is. banned and offering.

~

i'd been driving, no by then i was walking, and i almost
missed it. but i requires you, Luce, she is whispering, i am
whispering, into your hair. having climbed out of the taxi,
the argument with the men about the unfair share i was
supposed to be paying, or maybe it was she, as if i were
some other me, some mother me before i saw where i was
heading.

but i can't say she because that's not true either.

you're everything in the dream, you say. i'm your place
too? in dreams places are the architecture of souls. then

why did i dream yours destroyed? it wasn't quite destroyed, there were the owls. yes, there were the owls, but why owls? perhaps you're afraid.

can we disentangle this so i can tell it but telling is always one after another which is not the way we realize. and i didn't understand when Eleni said mythological.

putting my mouth very close to yours our lips are all mixed up with words: i'm walking home but it's unfamiliar territory and i'm coming from the place i got dropped off, miles off, and then i'm walking down your block when i see, my god, your place has been demolished. they've taken a bulldozer to it and it's just a pile of rubble, studs leaning crazily against the cubbyholes of what were rooms, your rooms. and still i feel you there as if i could walk in on you. somebody's painted the rubble black and there's some graffiti i can't quite make out. and then i see the owls — on broken planks, in cubbyholes, somebody's set these owls, watchful and fluorescent.

the bird that howls, you said, owl with an h, an itch — looking intently into me — you know what that means?

you were shivering, with my arms around you you were shivering. but it wasn't the dream. it's not even a dream, this current that moves us beyond recognition. lips to lips

we ex-change what isn't words in circulation, though later
on in the street alone, the feel of you in my mouth, i re-
lease them at full shout, *women,* another, a double word.
women beside ourselves.   our fierceness our loyalty our
loving.

Acts of Passage

Nicole Brossard/Mauve

*La réalité est un sursis au-delà
et du réel lorsqu'on observe
en l'apparence virtuelle, courbes
de ceci qui ressemble combien de fois
les images : la bouche au féminin
dose de sens émotion dorsale*

les liens autour de l'évidence
graphies, bouches modulées mentales
et
du corps pour ancrer la réalité
for real

les avalanches et le bord de page

au bord: vitesse/équation

*   *il y a des pierres au bord de
la mer, des risques d'erreur et
l'encombrement du bruit des vagues.*

*il y a quand je pense «disissit»
langage qui reflue dans mes yeux
comme un horizon, bord de pensée :
réalité des bouches*

la peau et preuves à l'appui
penser que parfois
écrire leur ressemble
en des traits indécidables
fiction culture cortex
M   A   U   V   E

Daphne Marlatt/Mauve/a reading

Real that of the under-bent
curves of the virtual we take for real
a gap   delayed that-over-there   re-
semblance the images repeat
mouth in the feminine, dos(e)
of sense making a dorsal
commotion

chained leans on the evidence
on hand / writing   mouths
changing key, mental
or out to sea and
of the body's anchoring reality
for (the) **real**

avalanche and page edge

                            (carried over

bordering on: speed/equation

take some stones at the seabord,
hazards of miscalculation, blockage
of wave noise. take my thinking
«say'dbesayingsays»   language ebbs
in my eyes horizonlike,   thought's
border : mouth's reality

skin and its evidents

to think   to write
sometimes resembles in
undecidable features

fiction culture cortex

M   A   U   V   E

M   A   U   V   E

cortex fiction culture

stains the other
mew   maiwa   mauve
malva rose core text
fiction rings round
skin immersed in
resemblance takes
the stain, sense
roseblue in tissue re-
membering

Daphne Marlatt/Character

walks so as not to be seen in
her exact skin   characterized as
feminine   eyes creased
with the light ice slivers splay
the air   brilliant   blank she crosses
stop & go the mind's traffic snow
a gulf i rides as rain at sea a sea
not so much crossed as what
her body impress nearness then tests
going
          launches itself

in its element not in
character

«a mark»

~

born in name, I the undersigned
established character, given the
references of friends, confreres in
business, credit on tap, sign
this personage
                    a person portrayed

by himself

«instrument for branding»

~

in character, «consistent with» as if
character were company limited
a stake in the real whatever the going
conversation is

                a series of positions

drawn with finesse, finite in liability

liable everywhere & scarcely singular
she enters at all points unlimited
rupture of children trivia noise

she has no character meaning
indissoluble boundaries

        s/he:

            s plural in excess of he

«pointed stake»

~

take a character, write s
not the S-burn hide, not
property marked with belonging

S does not belong, goes beyond
herself in excess of
longing to leap
right out of her skin

shin (tooth) Ś
take hold, bite into

ᗯ   ﾐ   S   s

signor, sister, son, sire, soprano
more she had a stake in
biting through the traces left
across her body writing
you

Nicole Brossard/Jeu de lettres

elle s'avance de manière à
ne pas être vue dans
la peau exacte de la région du genre
féminin les yeux aux prises avec
l'éclat de glace de la lumière du pli
traverse le vide l'air étincelant
s'arrête et va l'aura du cerveau
un abîme î come une ride de pluie sur la mer
la mer non pas tellement traversée que chevauchée
son corps impression de proximité, elle vérifie
allant
        élan de soi s'élancer

dans ses éléments
noeud de genres

«signature»

née dans le nom, je soussignée
dans le genre établi, compte tenu
des références d'amis, confrères
en affaire, signe à crédit
ce personnage
         une personne décrite
         en son portrait
à l'écart

«marque déposée»

dans la lettre «conforme à la loi» comme si
la lettre était affaire de compagnie limitée
dans le réel quel que soit son déroulement
la conversation est
               une série de propositions
tracée avec finesse dans le fini de la responsabilité

fiable partout & à peine singulière
elle déclare la rupture en tout point illimitée
les enfants, le bruit anecdotique

elle est sans caractère signifiant
insoluble l/imite
      i/lle:
           ℓ plurielles dans l'excès de ce qu'il

«enjeu de pointe»

prends une lettre, écris *ℓ*
non pas ce *L* de brûlant brandon, non
qui soit exempte de toute appartenance

*L*n'a de dieu, n'a de lieu
va au-delà d' -même
en l'excès du désir de l'élan
sortir de sa peau

perce la (dent)elle
tu saisis, mords-y

Ɛ L le

sibylle si belle elfe ellipse, la lyre
elle a de plus tout intérêt à
couper court au vertige des vestiges
en travers de son corps écrivant
toi

Booking Passage

To write

gazing at trees, rocks, boats, we feel the boats rock waves
in our arms, these arms of land go out of focus up the pass,
ça gaze? things go okay? like us, "like ones," who come and
go in the watery sound a sailboat makes, no wind, engine
drone, and the wake rolls to us, eyes closed to avoid our
gazing (gauze of a certain hue — nothing distinct beyond
blue) we find how things are in each other's skin, undone
up close, we rock our ends in each other's surge, wake on
wake of desire's passing, shudders, shifts . . .

this is not the distinction of looking (long and fixed the
gaze) as in backward ("summer is over") or back at you ("i
want to memorize your face forever . . .") — thoughts up
the pass.

it's us who move into awake, finding our calling.

(Dis)spelling

the alphabet of fear, a current running just offshore, off
the edge of some clan pier which wasn't mine, the sinking
feel of footings underwater, ankle-deep on what remains,
afraid i'll drown, swept out (there was a broom) to sea.

close by two women wade, prosaic under sun umbrella,
hauling pigeons to sell. i too discover i can walk . . . deep
in this place that feels like history, old jossticks burning,
old offerings.

here on this once bombed island i re-enter my singular,
body alive in the halflight morning, in a rush of wings
(gone) the cooroo song (blue dove, blue vulnerable yearn-
ing). you call me and i am speechless. you call me and i am
still. out of this murmuring wreckage of names, old beach,
i am finding a new floor. miles off i walk in water feeling
the current, our swift magnetic current run, all around the
islands sinking in me and you.

Booking passage

this coming and going in the dark of early morning, snow scribbling its thawline round the house. we are under-cover, under a cover of white you unlock your door on this slipperiness.

to throw it off, this cover, this blank that halts a kiss on the open road. i kiss you anyway, and feel you veer toward me, red tail lights aflare at certain patches, certain turns my tongue takes, provocative.

we haven't even begun to write . . . sliding the in-between as the ferry slips its shoreline, barely noticeable at first, a gathering beat of engines in reverse, the shudder of the turn to make that long passage out —

the price for this.

we stood on the road in the dark. you closed the door so carlight wouldn't shine on us. our kiss reflected in snow, the name for this.

under the covers, morning, you take my scent, writing me into your cells' history. deep in our sentencing, i smell you home.

there is the passage. there is the *booking* — and our fear of this.

you, sliding past the seals inert on the log boom. you slide and they don't raise their heads. you are into our current now of going, not inert, not even gone as i lick you loose. there is a light beginning over the ridge of my closed eyes.

passage booked. i see you by the window shore slips by, you reading Venice our history is, that sinking feel, those footings under water. i nose the book aside and pull you forward gently with my lips.

a path, channel or duct. a corridor. a book and not a book. not *booked* but off the record. this.

irresistible melt of hot flesh. furline and thawline align your long wet descent.

nothing in the book says where we might head. my tongue in you, your body cresting now around, around this tip's lip-suck   surge   rush of your coming in other words.

we haven't even begun to write . . . what keeps us going, this rush of wingspread, this under (nosing in), this wine-dark blood flower. this rubbing between the word and our skin.

~

tell me, tell me where you are when the bush closes in, all heat a luxuriance of earth so heavy i can't breathe the sti-fling wall of prickly rose, skreek of mosquito poised . . . for the wall to break

the wall that isolates, that i so late to this: it doesn't, it slides apart — footings, walls, galleries, this island architecture

one layer under the other, memory a ghost, a guide, his-tolytic where the pain is stored, murmur, *mer-mère,* his-toricity stored in the tissue, text . . . a small boat, fraught. trying to cross distance, trying to find that passage (se-cret). in libraries where whole texts, whole persons have been secreted away.

original sin he said was a late overlay. and under that and under that? sweat pouring down, rivers of thyme and tuberose in the words that climb toward your scanning eyes

She shouts aloud, Come! we know it; / thousand-eared night repeats that cry / across the sea shining between us

~

this tracking back and forth across the white, this tearing of papyrus crosswise, this tearing of love in our mouths to leave our mark in the midst of rumour, coming out.

. . . to write in lesbian.

the dark swell of a sea that separates and beats against our joined feet, islands me in the night, fear and rage the isolate talking in my head. to combat this slipping away, of me, of you, the steps . . . what was it we held in trust, tiny as a Venetian bead, fragile as words encrusted with pearl, *mathetriai,* not-mother, hidden mentor, lost link?

to feel our age we stood in the road in the dark, we stood in the roads and it was this old, a ripple of water against the hull, a coming and going

we began with . . .

her drowned thyme and clover, fields of it heavy with dew our feet soak up, illicit hands cupped one in the other as carlights pick us out. the yell a salute. marked, we are elsewhere,

translated here . . .

like her, precisely on this page, this mark: *a thin flame runs under / my skin.* twenty-five hundred years ago, this trembling then. actual as that which wets our skin her words come down to us, a rush, poured through the blood, this coming and going among islands is.